A Charlie Brown Christmas

Peanuts® characters created and drawn
by Charles M. Schulz

Text adapted by Diane Namm
Background illustrations by Art and Kim Ellis

A GOLDEN BOOK · NEW YORK
Western Publishing Company, Inc., Racine, Wisconsin 53404

"I don't know, Linus. I just don't know," said Charlie Brown with a sigh.

"What's wrong, Charlie Brown?" asked Linus.

"It's Christmastime again," said Charlie Brown. "And every year the same thing happens. Everyone is full of cheer—everyone but me."

"Oh, Charlie Brown," said Linus impatiently. "You're the only person in the world who could be unhappy about a wonderful holiday like Christmas. Well, I happen to like Christmas, and I'm happy for whatever joy this holiday brings others," he added.

Linus started walking home.
"I guess you're right, Linus. See you tomorrow," Charlie Brown called. Then he slowly walked home by himself.

"I don't get it. This just doesn't seem fair," said Charlie
Brown as he checked his mailbox. "Why does everybody
else get Christmas cards?

"Look at that," he said as he noticed Snoopy reading
a card. "Even my own dog gets Christmas cards.

"It's not right," Charlie Brown said as he walked away. "Why do they have to make holidays like this? Instead of making me feel happy, Christmas just makes me feel like no one cares about me." He thought for a moment. Then he said, "I think I'll go to Lucy for some good advice."

Charlie Brown walked up to Lucy's advice booth.
"What seems to be your problem, Charlie Brown?"
asked Lucy.
"I haven't been feeling well lately," said Charlie Brown.
"In fact, I'm very sad," he began.

"Ahem," said Lucy. "Before we begin, would you mind paying for my advice? I need the money to buy myself a Christmas present I really want."

"Oh, good grief!" said Charlie Brown, sighing.

"Five cents, please," Lucy said.

Charlie Brown dropped a nickel into the box.

"Thank you," said Lucy. "Now, what's the trouble, Charlie Brown?"

"Well, the problem is that I'm unhappy all the time," replied Charlie Brown. "I know it's Christmas and I should be full of good cheer, but I'm not. It's the same thing every year! Instead of feeling happier than usual, I just feel worse. Nobody ever sends me Christmas cards, or invites me to Christmas parties, or asks me to go caroling. I just can't seem to find the right Christmas spirit," he said.

"I know exactly what you need, Charlie Brown," Lucy said. "You need a real Christmas project, something to make you feel like you're a part of Christmas. Would you like to be the director of the school's Christmas play?" she asked.

"Me? A director?" said Charlie Brown. "But I wouldn't know what to do!"

"It's easy!" said Lucy. "I'll help you. Meet me at the school at three o'clock."

Lucy and Charlie Brown began walking home.

"By the way, Charlie Brown," called Lucy, "I know just
how you feel. I never get anything out of Christmas
either. Just some stupid old toys or some silly old doll,"
she said.

"What do you really want out of Christmas, Lucy?"
Charlie Brown asked.

"Cash!" Lucy replied.

"Oh, good grief!" said Charlie Brown.

Then Snoopy walked by carrying a bunch of Christmas lights.

"I wonder what Snoopy is going to do with all those lights?" Charlie Brown asked himself.

As he slowly walked home Charlie Brown tried to figure out what he really wanted out of Christmas.

Lost in his thoughts, Charlie Brown almost walked right by Snoopy's doghouse. Snoopy had decorated his house with so many Christmas lights that Charlie Brown hardly recognized it.

"What's going on here?" Charlie Brown asked. Then he bent down to pick up a piece of paper that was lying on the ground beside the doghouse.

Charlie Brown read what was written on the paper.
"Find out what Christmas really means. Win lots of
money in the Christmas Lights and Display contest!

"Win lots of money! Is that the only reason for decorating a house with Christmas lights?" asked Charlie Brown in disbelief. "Good grief! My own dog thinks Christmas is a way of making money! Whatever happened to Christmas carols and the true spirit of Christmas?"

In despair, Charlie Brown went home. "Maybe my little
sister, Sally, can think of a way to help me feel better
about Christmas," he thought.

When he got home, Sally did have a lot to say about
Christmas, but it wasn't quite what Charlie Brown had in
mind.

"Where have you been, big brother?" Sally said as she ran up to Charlie Brown. "I need a favor. I want you to write a letter to Santa Claus for me. I'll tell you exactly what I want to say," she added.

Sally began her letter to Santa, speaking as fast as she
possibly could.

"Dear Santa, how are you? Did you have a nice year?
How are Mrs. Claus and the elves? I've been very good
this year, so I have a long list of presents. If it's all too
much trouble, you can just send me money."

"Send you money! Good grief!" Charlie Brown
couldn't believe his ears. "I can't take it anymore! Even
my baby sister thinks that Christmas means cash!" he
shouted.

Charlie Brown grabbed his coat and hat and headed out
into the cold winter world.

Charlie Brown walked and walked. He didn't understand his sister or Snoopy or Lucy. Did Christmas only mean money and prizes and presents? "There must be some way to show that Christmas means more," he said to himself. "Christmas should be about hope and joy and giving to others."

Then he thought for a moment. "Maybe Lucy's advice will help. I'll direct that Christmas play. I'll put in love and hope and all that stuff. I'll show them what Christmas really means," Charlie Brown decided as he headed for the school auditorium.

When Charlie Brown arrived, everyone in the play was waiting for him. Charlie Brown could tell he had a lot of work to do if he was ever going to get this Christmas play off the ground.

"Here he is now," Lucy called out. "The director of our Christmas play—Charlie Brown!"

"OK, everybody," Charlie Brown began, "we have a very important job to do here. We're going to put on a play that will show everyone the true spirit of Christmas. We're going to have joy, hope, and love in this play—all the things that Christmas is supposed to be about.

"What do you say? Am I right? Am I right?" Charlie
Brown asked with enthusiasm. No one answered. "Hey,
why isn't anyone listening to the director? That's one of
the first rules for being in a play. How else are we going to
finish all the things we have to do today?"

Then he turned to Lucy, and in his most official voice
Charlie Brown said, "Lucy, hand out the scripts, please."

Lucy walked over to each cast member. She handed them their scripts and told them what parts they were playing. She gave Linus his script last.

"You're going to play a shepherd, whether you like it or not," Lucy said. "So you'd better learn your lines, and get rid of that stupid blanket!" she added.

"This is one shepherd who's going to keep his trusty blanket with him," Linus said. Then he wrapped his blanket around his head. He looked like a real shepherd.

"All right, everyone. Listen to me," called out Charlie
Brown. "We're going to practice the scene at the inn."
But the cast members were too busy dancing and
talking among themselves. They weren't paying any
attention to Charlie Brown at all.
"What's going on here? Stop it!" shouted Charlie
Brown.
"What is it, Charlie Brown?" someone asked.
"Let's get to work!" he said. "Linus, I want you and
Sally to stand over there."

"What do you want Sally for?" Linus asked, afraid of Charlie Brown's answer.

"She's going to play your wife," Charlie Brown replied.

"Oh, good grief!" said Linus. "It's bad enough I have to be a stupid shepherd in this play without having Sally play my wife!"

Sally was quite happy to come over and stand with Linus. She had been hoping that Charlie Brown would pick her to be Linus's wife.

"Oh, isn't my sweet babboo adorable?" said Sally, giving Linus a very big hug.

"Rats!" said Linus from underneath his blanket.

"Doesn't anyone here understand what we're trying to do?" asked Charlie Brown.

"What do you mean, Charlie Brown?" asked Lucy.

"Nobody around here seems to have the right Christmas spirit," he answered. "All they care about is what parts they're playing. We should all be working together to show the true meaning of Christmas to the audience."

"Face it, Charlie Brown," said Lucy. "Nobody agrees with your silly ideas about the real spirit of Christmas."

But Charlie Brown didn't want to believe that.
"Wait a minute!" he said. "I know just what this play needs—a Christmas tree to put us all in the right mood. Come on, Linus, let's go out and get one!"

Linus and Charlie Brown got their coats and hats and headed for the Christmas tree sale.
"Make sure you get a really nice Christmas tree," said Lucy. "Something shiny and bright—pink and plastic," she suggested. "Try to do something right for a change, Charlie Brown."

Charlie Brown and Linus walked around and around
the Christmas tree lot, but Charlie Brown couldn't seem
to find the kind of tree he was looking for.

"Gee, Linus," he said, "they sure don't make
Christmas trees the way they used to."

Just then Charlie Brown spotted the tree he wanted. It
was the smallest tree on the lot, and most of its needles
had fallen off, but it was a real live tree.

"That's it! That's our tree!" Charlie Brown shouted
happily.

"I don't know, Charlie Brown," Linus said.
"Remember what Lucy said? I don't think that tree fits
the modern spirit of Christmas."

Charlie Brown wasn't listening. He went to gather up
the tree to take it back to the school.

"We found it!" said Charlie Brown when he and Linus returned to the school. "It's the perfect Christmas tree!" Then he proudly held up the tree for everyone to see.

"You call that scrawny little thing a tree?" Lucy sneered. "Can't you do anything right, Charlie Brown? That's not the kind of Christmas tree we need."

The other cast members agreed with Lucy.

"I guess I shouldn't have picked this tree," said Charlie Brown sadly. "I guess I don't really understand what Christmas is all about. Can anyone tell me what the true meaning of Christmas is?"

"I can, Charlie Brown," Linus said. Then he stepped to the front of the stage, and he quietly told the story of Christmas, the day the baby Jesus was born.

And there were in the same country shepherds abiding in the field, keeping watch over their flock by night.

And, lo, the angel of the Lord came upon them, and the glory of the Lord shone round about them; and they were sore afraid.

And the angel said unto them, Fear not: for, behold, I bring you good tidings of great joy, which shall be to all people.

For unto you is born this day in the city of David a Saviour, which is Christ the Lord.

And this shall be a sign unto you; Ye shall find the babe wrapped in swaddling clothes, lying in a manger.

And suddenly there was with the angel a multitude of the heavenly host praising God, and saying,

Glory to God in the highest, and on earth peace, good will toward men.

As Linus spoke one by one the cast members packed
up their books and left the stage. By the time Linus
finished his story, he and Charlie Brown were the only
ones left. Then Charlie Brown headed home, taking his
little Christmas tree with him.

"Linus is right. I won't let pink Christmas trees or dogs
who enter decoration contests ruin my Christmas," Charlie
Brown said as he passed Snoopy's doghouse.

"I'll just take this tree, and I'll make it the most
beautiful Christmas tree in the world," said Charlie
Brown.

Then Charlie Brown borrowed one of Snoopy's
Christmas ornaments and placed it on his little tree,
but the ornament was too heavy. The tree just bent right
over.

"Oh, no! I've killed it!" cried Charlie Brown. "I can't
even decorate a tree!" He left the tree and ran home.

Then Linus came along. He found the tree in the snow.
"You're not such a bad little tree," Linus said. "You
just need a little love."

One by one everyone else from the play came to the
tree. They began to help Linus decorate it. In no time at
all it looked just like a Christmas tree should.

"I think this was just the kind of tree Charlie Brown
was talking about," said Linus.

Just then Charlie Brown came back. He was sorry he
had left his little tree all alone in the snow.

"What's this? What's going on?" Charlie Brown said.
"Is that beautiful tree my little Christmas tree?" he asked
in surprise.

His friends smiled happily and nodded their heads.

"Merry Christmas, Charlie Brown!" Linus shouted
with joy.

Charlie Brown clasped his hands. He felt all warm and
happy inside.

"At last I feel like it's Christmas," Charlie Brown said.
"Merry Christmas to all, and to all a good night," he
added cheerfully as he and his friends began caroling.